I WENT TO THE ANIMAL FAIR

I Wer

the Animal Fair

A BOOK OF ANIMAL POEMS

SELECTED BY

William Cole

ILLUSTRATED BY *Colette Rosselli*

COLLINS ● WORLD

Published by William Collins + World Publishing Company

Published simultaneously in Canada by
Nelson, Foster & Scott Ltd.

Copyright © 1958 by William Cole
New Printing August 1975

Library of Congress Cataloging in Publication Data

Cole, William, 1919-   ed.
   I went to the animal fair.

   SUMMARY: A collection of thirty-five animal poems by Lear, Coatsworth, Milne, de la Mare, Aldis, and other notable poets.

   1. Animals—Juvenile poetry. [1. Animals—Poetry. 2. Poetry—Collections] I. Rosselli, Colette. II. Title.
[PZ8.3.C675Ib7]   821'.008'036   75-23020
ISBN 0-529-03530-8 lib. bdg.

COPYRIGHT ACKNOWLEDGMENTS

Abelard-Schuman, Ltd., for "Baby Chick" from *Runny Days, Sunny Days,* by Aileen Fisher, copyright, 1957, Aileen Fisher. Reprinted by permission of Abelard-Schuman, Ltd.

Appleton-Century-Crofts, Inc., for "The Giraffe and the Woman" from *Merry-Go-Round,* by Laura E. Richards, copyright, 1935, D. Appleton-Century Co., Inc. Reprinted by permission of Appleton-Century-Crofts, Inc.

Polly Chase, for her poem "I Stare at the Cow" from Child Life Magazine. Reprinted by permission of the author.

Alice B. Campbell, for her poem "Sally and Manda" from *Living Poetry,* edited by Horace J. McNeil and Dorothy S. Zimmer, published by Globe Book Company. Reprinted by permission of the author.

Coward-McCann, Inc., for "The Mouse" from *Compass Rose,* by Elizabeth Coatsworth, copyright, 1929, Coward-McCann, Inc.

The Cresset Press Limited, for "At Night" from *Spring Morning,* by Frances Cornford.

Doubleday & Co., Inc., for "The Animal Store" from *Taxis and Toadstools,* by Rachel Field, copyright, 1926, Doubleday & Co., Inc. Reprinted by permission of Doubleday & Co., Inc.

Animal Fair

I went to the animal fair,
The birds and beasts were there.
The big baboon by the light of the moon
Was combing his auburn hair.

The monkey he got drunk.
He stepped on the elephant's trunk.
The elephant sneezed
And fell on his knees,
And that was the end of the munk,
     the munk, the munk.
And that was the end of the munk.

Old rhyme

]

The House of the Mouse

The house of the mouse
is a wee little house,
a green little house in the grass,
which big clumsy folk
may hunt and may poke

and still never see as they pass
this sweet little, neat little,
wee little, green little,
cuddle-down hide-away
house in the grass.

Lucy Sprague Mitchell

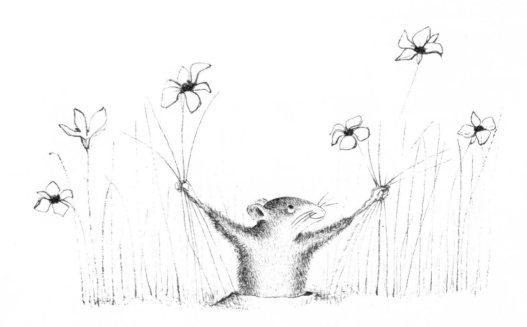

from *A Bird*

A bird came down the walk:
He did not know I saw;
He bit an angle-worm in halves
And ate the fellow, raw.

And then he drank a dew
From a convenient grass,
And then hopped sidewise to the wall
To let a beetle pass.

Emily Dickinson

Frogs at School

Twenty froggies went to school
Down beside a rushy pool;
Twenty little coats of green,
Twenty vests all white and clean.

"We must be in time," said they
"First we study, then we play;
That is how we keep the rule,
When we froggies go to school."

Master Bullfrog, grave and stern,
Called the classes in their turn;
Taught them how to nobly strive,
Likewise how to leap and dive.

From his seat upon a log,
Showed them how to say, "Ker-chog!"
Also how to dodge a blow
From the sticks which bad boys throw.

Twenty froggies grew up fast;
Bullfrogs they became at last.
Not one dunce was in the lot,
Not one lesson they forgot.

Polished in a high degree,
As each froggy ought to be,
Now they sit on other logs,
Teaching other little frogs.

George Cooper

The Mysterious Cat

I saw a proud, mysterious cat,
I saw a proud, mysterious cat
Too proud to catch a mouse or rat—
Mew, mew, mew.

But catnip she would eat, and purr,
But catnip she would eat, and purr.
And goldfish she did much prefer—
Mew, mew, mew.

I saw a cat—'twas but a dream,
I saw a cat—'twas but a dream,
Who scorned the slave that brought her cream—
Mew, mew, mew.

Unless the slave were dressed in style,
Unless the slave were dressed in style,
And knelt before her all the while—
Mew, mew, mew.

Did you ever hear of a thing like that?
Did you ever hear of a thing like that?
Did you ever hear of a thing like that?
Oh, what a proud, mysterious cat.
Oh, what a proud, mysterious cat.
Oh, what a proud, mysterious cat.
Mew . . . mew . . . mew.

Vachel Lindsay

[1

Foal

Come trotting up
Beside your mother,
Little skinny.

Lay your neck across
Her back, and whinny,
Little foal.

You think you're a horse
Because you can trot—
But you're not.

Your eyes are so wild,
And each leg is as tall
As a pole;

And you're only a skittish
Child, after all,
Little foal.

Mary Britton Miller

Quack!

The duck is whiter than whey is,
His tail tips up over his back,
The eye in his head is as round as a button,
And he says, *Quack! Quack!*

He swims on his bright blue mill-pond,
By the willow tree under the shack,
Then stands on his head to see down to the bottom,
And says, *Quack! Quack!*

When Mollie steps out of the kitchen,
For apron—pinned round with a sack;
He squints at her round face, her dish, and what's
And says, *Quack! Quack!*

He preens the pure snow of his feathers
In the sun by the wheat-straw stack;
At dusk waddles home with his brothers and siste
And says, *Quack! Quack!*

Walter de la

[1

The Giraffe and the Woman

Sing a song of laughter
   About the young giraffter
Who tried to reach the rafter
   To get the apple-pie;
The woman put it there, you know,
'Cause she was in despair, you know,
"He reaches everywhere, you know,
   And eats until I *cry!*"

Sing a song of laughter!
The greedy young giraffter,
He got what he was after,
   And it was piping hot!
It burnt his mouth so terribly,
He yelped and yammered yerribly,
The woman chuckled merribly,
   And said, "See what you got!"

            Laura E. Richards

The Tale of a Dog

When my little dog is happy,
  And canine life is bliss,
He always keeps his joyful tail

        s
        i
        h
        t
        e
        k
        i

A-standing up l

When my little dog is doleful,
  And bones are scarce, you know,
He always keeps his mournful tail
  A-hanging 'way d

        o
        w
        n
        l
        o
        w
        .

James H. Lambert, Jr.

Old Hogan's Goat

Old Hogan's goat was feeling fine,
Ate six red shirts from off the line;
Old Hogan grabbed him by the back
And tied him to the railroad track.
Now when the train came into sight,
That goat grew pale and green with fright;
He heaved a sigh, as if in pain,
Coughed up those shirts and flagged the train!

Nonsense song

Five Eyes

In Hans' old mill his three black cats
Watch his bins for the thieving rats.
Whisker and claw, they crouch in the night,
Their five eyes smouldering green and bright:
Squeaks from the flour sacks, squeaks from where
The cold wind stirs on the empty stair,
Squeaking and scampering, everywhere.
Then down they pounce, now in, now out,
At whisking tail, and sniffing snout;
While lean old Hans he snores away
Till peep of light at break of day;
Then up he climbs to his creaking mill,
Out come his cats all grey with meal—
Jekkel, and Jessup, and one-eyed Jill.

Walter de la Mare

The Owl

The Owl that lives in the old oak tree
Opens his eyes and cannot see
When it's clear as day to you and me;
But not long after the sun goes down
And the Church Clock strikes in Tarrytown
And Nora puts on her green nightgown,
He opens his big bespectacled eyes
And shuffles out of the hollow tree,
And flies and flies

                 and flies and flies,

And flies and flies

                 and flies and flies.

William Jay Smith

Eletelephony

Once there was an elephant,
Who tried to use the telephant—
No! no! I mean an elephone
Who tried to use the telephone—
(Dear me! I am not certain quite
That even now I've got it right.)

Howe'er it was, he got his trunk
Entangled in the telephunk;
The more he tried to get it free,
The louder buzzed the telephee—
(I fear I'd better drop the song
Of elephop and telephong!)

Laura E. Richards

If You Ever

If you ever ever ever ever ever
   If you ever ever ever meet a whale
You must never never never never never
   You must never never never touch its tail:
For if you ever ever ever ever ever,
   If you ever ever ever touch its tail,
You will never never never never never,
   You will never never meet another whale.

Unknown

The Grasshoppers

High
Up
Over the top
Of feathery grasses the
Grasshoppers hop.
They won't eat their suppers;
They will not obey
Their grasshopper mothers
And fathers, who say:
"Listen, my children,
This must be stopped—
Now is the time your last
Hop should be hopped;
So come eat your suppers
And go to your beds—"

But the little green grasshoppers
Shake their green heads.
"No,
No—"
The naughty ones say,
"All we have time to do
Now is to play.
If we want supper we'll
Nip at a fly
Or nibble a blueberry
As we go by;
If we feel sleepy we'll
Close our eyes tight
And snoozle away in a
Harebell all night.
But not
Now.
Now we must hop.
And nobody,
NOBODY,
Can make us stop."

Dorothy Aldis

Furry Bear

If I were a bear,
　And a big bear too,
I shouldn't much care
　If it froze or snew;
I shouldn't much mind
　If it snowed or friz—
I'd be all fur-lined
　With a coat like his!

For I'd have fur boots and a brown fur wrap,
And brown fur knickers and a big fur cap.
I'd have a fur muffle-ruff to cover my jaws,
And brown fur mittens on my big brown paws.
With a big brown furry-down up to my head,
I'd sleep all the winter in a big fur bed.

A. A. Milne

]

A Cat May Look at a King

The Cat
  Came and sat
  Down before His Majesty;
The Cat
Came and sat
  Down before the King.
"I've come to take a look,
For unless I am mistook,
It is written in a book,
  I may do this thing!"

She took
Quite a look,
    Over all His Majesty;
She took
Quite a look,
    And then she shook her head.
"There's little here to praise,
Plain his looks and dull his ways;
I'll turn my loving gaze
    On Tabby Tom instead!"

Laura E. Richards

The Snare

I hear a sudden cry of pain!
   There is a rabbit in a snare:
Now I hear the cry again,
   But I cannot tell from where.

But I cannot tell from where
   He is calling out for aid;
Crying on the frightened air,
   Making everything afraid.

Making everything afraid,
   Wrinkling up his little face,
As he cries again for aid;
   And I cannot find the place!

And I cannot find the place
   Where his paw is in the snare:
Little one! Oh, little one!
   I am searching everywhere.

James Stephens

The Mouse

I heard a mouse
Bitterly complaining
In a crack of moonlight
Aslant on the floor—

"Little I ask
And that little is not granted.
There are few crumbs
In this world any more.

"The bread-box is tin
And I cannot get in.

"The jam's in a jar
My teeth cannot mar.

"The cheese sits by itself
On the pantry shelf.

"All night I run
Searching and seeking,
All night I run
About on the floor.

"Moonlight is there
And a bare place for dancing,
But no little feast
Is spread any more."

Elizabeth Coatsworth

The Owl and the Pussy-Cat

The Owl and the Pussy-Cat went to sea
  In a beautiful pea-green boat,
They took some honey, and plenty of money
  Wrapped up in a five-pound note.
The Owl looked up to the stars above,
  And sang to a small guitar,
"O lovely Pussy! O Pussy, my love,
  What a beautiful Pussy you are,
     You are,
     You are!
What a beautiful Pussy you are!"

Pussy said to the Owl, "You elegant fowl!
  How charmingly sweet you sing!
O let us be married! too long we have tarried:
  But what shall we do for a ring?"
They sailed away for a year and a day,
  To the land where the Bong-tree grows,
And there in a wood a Piggy-wig stood,
  With a ring at the end of his nose,
     His nose,
     His nose,
With a ring at the end of his nose.

"Dear Pig, are you willing to sell for one shilling
    Your ring?" Said the Piggy, "I will."
So they took it away, and were married next day
    By the Turkey who lives on the hill.
They dined on mince, and slices of quince,
    Which they ate with a runcible spoon;
And hand in hand, on the edge of the sand,
    They danced by the light of the moon,
        The moon,
        The moon,
    They danced by the light of the moon.

Edward Lear

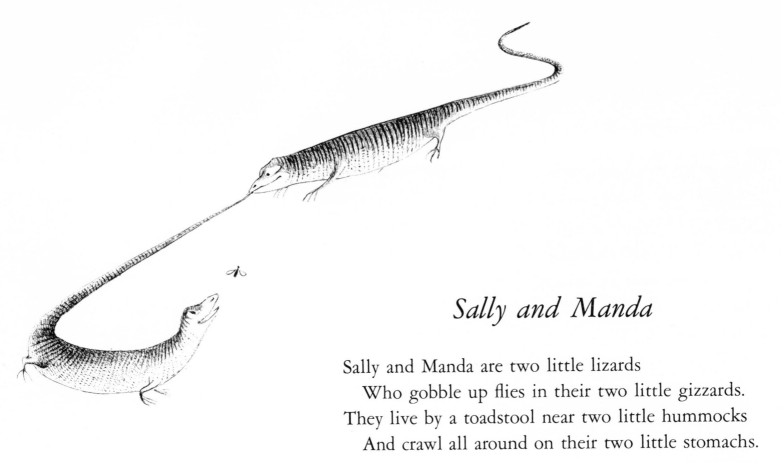

Sally and Manda

Sally and Manda are two little lizards
   Who gobble up flies in their two little gizzards.
They live by a toadstool near two little hummocks
   And crawl all around on their two little stomachs.

Alice B. Campbell

The Milkman's Horse

On summer mornings when it's hot,
The milkman's horse can't even trot;
But pokes along like this—
Klip-klop, Klip-klop, Klip-klop.

But in the winter brisk,
He perks right up and wants to frisk;
And then he goes like this—
Klippty-klip, Klippty-klip, Klippty-klip.

Unknown

The Cat's Tea-Party

Five little pussy-cats, invited out to tea,
Cried: "Mother, let us go—Oh, do! for good we'll surely be.
We'll wear our bibs and hold our things as you have shown us how—
Spoons in right paws, cups in left—and make a pretty bow;
We'll always say 'Yes, if you please,' and 'Only half of that.' "
"Then go, my darling children," said the happy Mother Cat.
The five little pussy-cats went out that night to tea,
Their heads were smooth and glossy, their tails were swinging free;
They held their things as they had learned, and tried to be polite;—
With snowy bibs beneath their chins they were a pretty sight.

But, alas, for manners beautiful, and coats as soft as silk!
The moment that the little kits were asked to take some milk,
They dropped their spoons, forgot to bow, and—oh, what do you think?
They put their noses in the cups and all began to drink!
Yes, every naughty little kit set up a miou for more,
Then knocked the tea-cups over, and scampered through the door.

F. E. Weatherley

Baby Chick

Peck
  peck
   peck
on the warm brown egg.
OUT comes a neck.
OUT comes a leg.

How
  does
   a chick,
who's not been about,
discover the trick
of how to get out?

Aileen Fisher

The Jolly Woodchuck

The woodchuck's very very fat
But doesn't care a pin for that.

When nights are long and the snow is deep,
Down in his hole he lies asleep.

Under the earth is a little warm room
The drowsy woodchuck calls his home.

Rolls of fat and fur surround him,
With all his children curled around him,

Snout to snout and tail to tail.
He never wakes in the wildest gale;

When icicles snap and the north wind blows
He snores in his sleep and rubs his nose.

Marion Edey and *Dorothy Grider*

The Camel's Complaint

"Canary-birds feed on sugar and seed,
   Parrots have crackers to crunch;
And as for the poodles, they tell me the noodles
   Have chickens and cream for their lunch.
     But there's never a question
     About MY digestion—
     ANYTHING does for me!

"Cats, you're aware, can repose in a chair,
   Chickens can roost upon rails;
Puppies are able to sleep in a stable,
   And oysters can slumber in pails.
     But no one supposes
     A poor Camel dozes—
     ANY PLACE does for me!

"Lambs are enclosed where it's never exposed,
 Coops are constructed for hens;
Kittens are treated to houses well heated,
 And pigs are protected by pens.
  But a Camel comes handy
  Wherever it's sandy—
ANYWHERE does for me!

"People would laugh if you rode a giraffe,
 Or mounted the back of an ox;
It's nobody's habit to ride on a rabbit,
 Or try to bestraddle a fox.
  But as for a Camel, he's
  Ridden by families—
ANY LOAD does for me!

"A snake is as round as a hole in the ground,
 And weasels are wavy and sleek;
And no alligator could ever be straighter
 Than lizards that live in a creek.
  But a Camel's all lumpy
  And bumpy and humpy—
ANY SHAPE does for me!"

Charles E. Carryl

I Had a Dove

I had a dove and the sweet dove died;
   And I have thought it died of grieving:
O what could it grieve for? Its feet were tied,
   With a silken thread of my own hand's weaving;
   Sweet little red feet! why should you die—
Why should you leave me, sweet bird! Why?
You lived alone in the forest-tree,
Why, pretty thing! would you not live with me?
I kissed you oft and gave you white peas;
Why not live sweetly, as in the green trees?

John Keats

Another in his strawy lair
Says: "Who's a-howling over there?
By heavens, I will stop him soon
From interfering with the moon!"

So back he barks, with throat upthrown:
"You leave our moon, our moon alone!"
And other distant dogs respond
Beyond the fields, beyond, beyond. . . .

Frances Cornford

At Night

On moony nights the dogs bark shrill
Down the valley and up the hill.

There's one is angry to behold
The moon so unafraid and cold,
Who makes the earth as bright as day,
But yet unhappy, dead, and gray.

I Stare at the Cow

I stare at the cow
And
The cow stares at me.
I do not bow.
It would start a row
To bow
To a cow!

I think it is safer to let her be,
Munching and crunching
S-O S-L--E---E--P--I--L-Y.

But look at her now!
What a different cow!
She's beginning to bow!

So I RUN for a tree!

Polly Chase

Missing

Has anybody seen my mouse?

I opened his box for half a minute,
Just to make sure he was really in it,
And while I was looking, he jumped outside!
I tried to catch him, I tried, I tried. . . .
I think he's somewhere about the house.
Has *anyone* seen my mouse?

Uncle John, have you seen my mouse?

Just a small sort of mouse, a dear little brown one,
He came from the country, he wasn't a town one,
So he'll feel all lonely in a London street;
Why, what could he possibly find to eat?

He must be somewhere. I'll ask Aunt Rose:
Have *you* seen a mouse with a woffelly nose?
Oh, somewhere about—
He's just got out. . . .

Hasn't *anybody* seen my mouse?

A. A. Milne

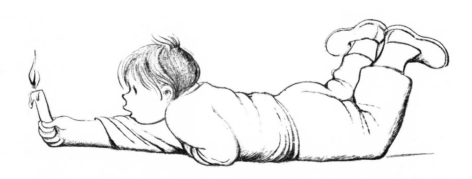

The Chameleon

The chameleon changes his color;
    He can look like a tree or a wall;
He is timid and shy and he hates to be seen,
So he simply sits down on the grass and grows green,
    And pretends he is nothing at all.

I wish I could change my complexion
    To purple or orange or red:
I wish I could look like the arm of a chair
So nobody ever would know I was there
    When they wanted to put me to bed.

I wish I could be a chameleon
    And look like a lily or rose;
I'd lie on the apples and peaches and pears,
But not on Aunt Margaret's yellowy chairs—
    I should have to be careful of those.

The chameleon's life is confusing;
    He is used to adventure and pain;
But if ever he sat on Aunt Maggie's cretonne
And found what a curious color he'd gone,
    I don't think he'd do it again.

A. P. Herbert

The Animal Store

If I had a hundred dollars to spend,
  Or maybe a little more,
I'd hurry as fast as my legs would go
  Straight to the animal store.

I wouldn't say, "How much for this or that?"—
  "What kind of a dog is he?"
I'd buy as many as rolled an eye,
  Or wagged a tail at me!

I'd take the hound with the drooping ears
  That sits by himself alone;
Cockers and Cairns and wobbly pups
  For to be my very own.

I might buy a parrot all red and green,
  And the monkey I saw before,
If I had a hundred dollars to spend,
  Or maybe a little more.

Rachel Field

Butterfly

Of living creatures most I prize
Black-spotted yellow Butterflies
Sailing softly through the skies,

Whisking light from each sunbeam,
Gliding over field and stream—
Like fans unfolding in a dream,

Like fans of gold lace flickering
Before a drowsy elfin king
For whom the thrush and linnet sing—

Soft and beautiful and bright
As hands that move to touch the light
When Mother leans to say good night.

William Jay Smith

Title Index

Author Index